Disney • PIXAR

a bug's life

Flik's Perfect Gift

Judy Katschke

Disney's First Readers — Level 2
A Story from Disney/Pixar's *A Bug's Life*

Disney PRESS

New York

It is Queen Atta's birthday.
All the ants are bringing gifts!

But what's bugging Flik?

"I want to bring the *perfect* gift!"
Flik says.

Flik looks high.
Flik looks low.

Finding the perfect gift
is no picnic!

Flik thinks and thinks.
"I've got it!" he cries.

Flik's ideas start to bloom!

"It's just a plain old daisy now,"
Flik says. "But soon it will be..."

"A merry-go-round for Atta!
Come on, Dot, let's try it out!"

WHOOPS!

"Maybe Atta can use a nice, cool breeze!

Get ready to chill, Dot!"

WHOOSH!

"Or how about a new way for Atta to fly?

Hop on, Dot!"

"Maybe you should just get Atta a card," Dot says.
"I will not give up," Flik cries.
"I *will* find the perfect present!"

"I'll build her a beach umbrella!"
Flik says. "A sprinkler! A ferris wheel!"

Uh-oh. It's Queen Atta!

"What's that, Flik?" Queen Atta asks.

"It's just a plain old daisy," Flik says.
"It's *perfect*," Queen Atta cries.

"It is?" Flik asks. He looks
at the daisy and smiles. "It *is*!
Happy birthday, Atta!"